WEBSITE OF THE
CRACKED COOKIES

YA
K

WEBSITE OF THE
CRACKED COOKIES

BY **ERIC A. KIMMEL**

ILLUSTRATED BY **JEFF SHELLY**

DUTTON CHILDREN'S BOOKS NEW YORK

To Lisa
E.A.K.

For my wife, Christine
J.S.

Text copyright © 2001 by Eric A. Kimmel
Illustrations copyright © 2001 by Jeff Shelly

Library of Congress Cataloging-in-Publication Data
Kimmel, Eric A.
Website of the cracked cookies / by Eric A. Kimmel;
illustrated by Jeff Shelly.—1st ed. p. cm.
Sequel to: Website of the warped wizard.
Summary: While trying to play the games at a seemingly harmless Website,
Jess and her friend Matt are sucked into a cyberworld filled with characters
from familiar fairy tales, all controlled by the evil Granny Goose.
ISBN 0-525-46799-8
[1. Computer games—Fiction. 2. Characters in literature—Fiction.]
I. Shelly, Jeff, ill. II. Title.   PZ7.K5648 Wd 2001 [Fic]—dc21 2001028304

Published in the United States by Dutton Children's Books,
a division of Penguin Putnam Books for Young Readers
345 Hudson Street, New York, New York 10014
www. penguinputnam.com

Designed by Alan Carr · Printed in USA · First Edition
10 9 8 7 6 5 4 3 2 1

CONTENTS

WEBSITE OF THE
Cracked Cookies

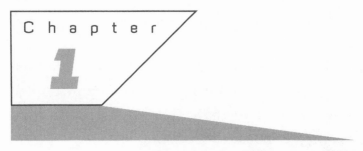

Gunning for Gradys

Click . . . click . . . click . . .

Images flickered across the ninety-inch, high-density, living-color television screen. Breakfast cereal, laxatives, cartoon characters, politicians, rock stars, wrestlers, athletes, supermodels . . .

Click . . . click . . . click . . .

"Just my luck! Two hundred eighty-seven channels and nothing to watch," Jessica Lyons grumbled as she stretched out on the recliner in the family room. She pointed the channel clicker at the enormous TV set filling the opposite wall.

"Here's the story . . . of a man named Grady—!" *CLICK!*

"The Lord wants to help you. Really he does! But first you gotta show you have faith. How do you show the Lord you have faith? Send your check to me, Brother Bob, at—" *CLICK!*

"I love you, you love me, we're a happy family—" *CLICK!*

"I promise that if elected—" *CLICK!*

"Crikey! The crocs are eating the hippo! This is the most exciting day of my life! Uh-oh! One of the crocs is turning around. I think he sees me—" *CLICK!*

"Well, Oprah, after the crocodiles ate my husband, I decided it was time for a makeover—" *CLICK!*

"Jessica? Did you do all the chores? Did you walk the dog? Did you empty the cat box? Did you finish your homework?" *CLICK!*

"Don't click me! I'm not a TV show! I'm your mother! Did you hear what I said? I asked if you got the chores done. I left a list for you on the refrigerator. Did you read it?"

Jessica swiveled around in her chair. Her mom

stood by the doorway. She had just gotten home from the hospital and was still wearing her scrubs. She must have been standing in the doorway awhile because her face was red and she looked angry. Jessica's mom was not a person who liked being ignored. Or clicked, like a boring guest on a talk show.

"Sorry, Mom, I didn't hear you come in. Yeah, I read the list. Everything's done. I even emptied out the cat box and put in fresh kitty litter. Now I'm relaxing after a hard, hard day."

"You don't know the meaning of 'hard,' honey. Wait till you have kids and a job. What are you watching?"

"Some supermodel. She's talking about her nose. She thinks it's too big. Is my nose too big, Mom?" Jessica fingered her own honker. "Do you think I need plastic surgery?"

"No, you don't need plastic surgery," Jessica's mom said. "Your nose is exactly the right size for your face. And so is that young woman's. As long as she keeps dressing like that, she doesn't have to worry about her nose—nobody's going to look at it. Frankly, honey, I don't like the way these people on

TV influence your thinking. They try to make you believe that if you don't look a certain way or dress a certain way, you don't count. Why can't you just be yourself?"

"Okay, Mom. I'll be myself," Jess said. "And right now my self wants to watch more TV."

"And my self wants you to turn the TV off and do something else."

"But, Mom, I might miss something!" Jessica whined.

"Trust me, hon. You won't miss a thing. And if you do, you can always catch the reruns."

"Can I play computer games?"

"I don't know, Jess—"

"I do. Bye!" Jessica clicked off the TV and ran up the stairs to her room. Within minutes her computer was online and humming. The sound effects coming through the speakers shook the walls.

KA-BLAM! KA-BLAM! KA-CHUNG!

BOOM! BOOM! BOOM! BOOM!

POW! POW! POW! POW! POW! POW! POW! POW! POW!

BUDDA-BUDDA-BUDDA! EEEEEEEEEEEE—WHUMP!

The noise was so loud that Jessica didn't hear her mom come in. "Is that a new game . . . I ASKED YOU, IS THAT A NEW GAME?!"

"Chill, Mom! You don't have to yell." Jess's on-screen character slapped another clip into her AK-47. "I downloaded it off the Web while I finished my chores. Everybody in school is talking about it. It comes from a terrific gaming site called Sitcom Showdown. Matt turned me on to it."

Matthew was Jessica's A-Number-1 cyber-pal. They shared games, videos, downloads. They also went on cyber-adventures together.

"The site lets you play all these video games using characters from your favorite TV shows," Jessica explained. "This one is Gradys Go Ballistic. The Grady Bunch has been together too long. They have all these people who never really liked each other living in this one little house. One day they just lose it. You get to choose your character and your weapon. I'm Marcia, and I chose an automatic assault rifle. Just a sec, Mom." Jessica's Marcia raked the kitchen. "Ahhh! I'm dead!" someone screamed. A teenage boy tumbled out of the pantry, riddled with bullets. "Gotcha, Greg! Serves you right. I told you to leave the Oreos alone." Jessica turned to her mom. "See? What did I tell you? It's incredibly cool!"

"Don't you think it's a little violent?"

"No, Mom! It's only a game. It isn't real. The Gradys can't hurt me, and I can't hurt them because they're reruns. Reruns never die. They go on forever. Like Gilligan."

"I suppose there's a *Gilligan's Island* game, too."

"Oh, yeah! Gilligan's Island Gumbo. The coconuts run out, and there's nothing to eat, so all the castaways on the island become cannibals. The trick is to get the Skipper first. He's the fattest. He'll give you the extra energy to take on the others. Ginger's a waste of time. No meat on her at all. The website has tons of games, Mom. Lucy and Desi Death Match, South Park Slaughter, Simpson Survivors . . . " Jessica counted the choices on her fingers.

"Do I understand this? There's a website that lets kids put their favorite television characters in a game so they can kill them?"

Jessica paused. "Well, it's not like they're totally defenseless."

"Honey, I'm really worried about your fascination with violent computer games." Jessica's mom spoke in her "concerned health-care professional" voice, the one she used at the hospital when interviewing people with strange diseases that were (a) highly contagious, (b) potentially fatal, (c) probably incurable, and (d) all of the above. "Today we had a staff meeting about the effect of computer games on children's physical and mental health. In its final stages CGCD, or Computer Game Compulsive Disorder, results in devastating symptoms. Nerve cells cease to function; mental processes shut down. The brain itself begins to dissolve. In the end it turns into a viscous substance resembling blueberry yogurt."

Jessica shuddered. She despised blueberry yogurt. "But Mom, I love playing computer games. They're fun! They're challenging. They teach you how to think. Look, if I didn't know that Alice was compulsive about mopping the kitchen floor, I never would have seen Greg's footprints leading to the pantry. That could have been me—Marcia Grady—bleeding on the linoleum! I love computer games. I can't give them up. What else am I supposed to do for fun? Watch TV?"

Jessica's mom spoke calmly and deliberately, the way she spoke when she had already made up her mind. "I'm not asking you to give up computer games completely. And I certainly am not suggesting television as an alternative. However, I think it might be a good idea for you to try exploring some different games. Games that don't involve violence."

"I don't know any nonviolent games," Jessica protested. "Even in Arthur's Math Blaster you still have to shoot down the numbers!"

"That's a good point. It came up at our meeting," Jessica's mom replied. "Contrary to what most gamers believe, we learned that there are many nonviolent games. They can be just as exciting and challenging as the others. We learned about a whole website featuring interactive, nonviolent games that are loads of fun to play. I wrote it down. We can log on now."

"But Mom, I'm in the middle of a game!"

"I think you and the Gradys need a break from each other. Send the Gradys to family counseling. You and I are going to . . ." Jessica's mom leaned over the desk and tapped the website address out on the keyboard:

<www.grannysworld.com>

Butterflies filled Jessica's stomach as she watched the website loading. This was worse than taking on an army of Gradys. Jessica's heart sank as she read the title filling her monitor screen.

GRANNY GOOSE'S FUN FARM

Scrolling down, she saw a computer-enhanced image of a tiny old lady in a calico dress standing in the doorway of a gingerbread house. Rinky-tinky music began to play. Grinning computer-animated squirrels, cuddly rabbits, and fluffy kittens tumbled on a green lawn edged with singing smiley-face flowers.

"Everybody's coming to Granny's Fun Farm!
Granny's Fun Farm! Granny's Fun Farm!"

"Mom, I can't do this! It's humiliating."

"There's nothing humiliating about learning to enjoy positive, challenging, multicultural, nonviolent computer games." Jessica's mom replied. "Try it. That's all I ask. You can do it, honey. Give it a chance. And I'm going to make sure you give it a chance. Because I'm going to take all your other computer and video games and lock them in the downstairs closet."

Jessica panicked. "Mom! That's not fair! Don't leave me like this! I'll do twice as many chores! I'll paint the house! I'll fix the roof! I'll scoop out the cat box with my bare hands!"

Jessica's mother gave Jess a kiss on the cheek as she left the room, taking the box of Jess's favorite games with her. "Love you!"

Jess couldn't answer. She watched as the herky-jerky computer movie began to play. Granny Goose and her cuddly pals danced and sang along with the smiley flowers as Jessica's eyes widened. Her mouth dropped open, but no sound escaped her throat. Granny Goose's Fun Farm had to be the worst game site ever created. And she was trapped in it, like a prisoner in a dungeon. Like a sailor marooned on a desert island. Like Marcia Grady at a rap concert.

"Help!" she squeaked. There had to be someone who could rescue her from a fate worse than reruns.

She checked to see if any of her friends were online. Matt was. "I'm in luck!" she exclaimed. She sent him a quick message. **Come over quick! I'm in trouble.**

I'll be right there, Matt wrote back.

Chapter 2

No Fun Farm

"I don't think it's so bad," Matt said, looking over Jess's shoulder at the monitor. He hummed the Fun Farm song as the movie ran a second time.

"Did you fall off your bike on your way over?" Jess asked. "I think you've suffered serious brain damage. We'd better get you to the hospital for X rays."

"There's nothing wrong with my brain. I just disagree with you, Jess," Matt said. "I don't think this website is so terrible."

"Harvey Hamster's Happy Hole? Sing Along with Susie Sunflower? Learn Spanish with Carlotta

the Cow? Excuse me—Carlotta la Vaca! Crabcakes!
It's so awful, it's toxic!" Jess pounded her fists
against her forehead, as if she had a terrible head-
ache.

"Tell your mom you don't want to do it. You'd
rather read a book. She's not going to object to
that," Matt suggested.

"I read all the Harry Potters."

"There are other books."

"No, there aren't. Come on, Matt! Think of
something!"

"What about your dad?"

"Forget it. He'll try to talk me into joining some
soccer team."

"What's wrong with soccer?" Matt asked.

"Too violent," Jess replied.

"Soccer is violent?"

"Haven't you seen the parents at a league cham-
pionship? It's a wonder anyone gets off the field
alive!"

"I'm stumped. I don't know what else to suggest.
You could turn your mom in for child abuse."

Jess squashed that idea. "They'd throw the book
at her for making me play this game. Serial killers

would get out of jail before she did. I can't let that happen to my mom. She means well. It's just that she doesn't know anything about computer games."

"I think you're making too big a deal of this, Jess. Okay, the website is a little juvenile. So what? That just means the games and puzzles are going to be easy to solve. It can't be any harder than putting together those wooden jigsaw puzzles in kindergarten. How long can it take? Five minutes? You'll explore the website, play the games, solve the mysteries, sing the songs, and you're done! Type in your mom's name and her e-mail address at work so she'll get all the spam this is sure to generate. I guarantee she'll never force you to play another online game again. What can she say? You'll have done everything she asked you to do. She'll have to give back your games. You'll be home free!"

Jess looked skeptical. "Are you sure I can be done and out in five minutes?"

"Of course I'm sure!" Matt exclaimed. "Have I ever been wrong?"

"I'm not going to answer that. Okay. Here we go." Jess moved the cursor to the smiley sunflower with <Enter> across its teeth and clicked.

The monitor went black. Jess's room began spinning around. She and Matt found themselves whirling in circles, like Toto and Dorothy in the cyclone on their way to Oz.

"Oh no!" Jess wailed. "It's one of these!"

"Oops!" said Matt.

Jess and Matt opened their eyes. The surrounding landscape looked as if it had come out of Munchkinland, if Munchkinland had been generated by a computer. They walked across the lime green grass, stopped by the edge of the aqua lake to watch the bright pink flamingos wading in the shallows.

"They look like lawn ornaments," Jess remarked.

"It's plastic!" Matt exclaimed, bending down to touch a dandelion. "Everything's plastic here!"

"Who are you calling 'plastic,' punk?" the dandelion sneered.

"Yeah! Watch your mouth!" a raccoon called from a tree.

"Cool your jets!" Jess shot back. "Nobody's talking to you. It's none of your business."

"I'll come down from this tree and make it my business," the raccoon said.

"Oh yeah? Keep it up, buddy, and I'll tell Davy Crockett where you live."

Matt took Jess's arm and hurried her down the yellow plastic road before a fight started. "Let's go. We don't want to cause trouble."

"He started it," Jess insisted. "We don't have to take that from a rodent."

"Raccoons aren't rodents. They're related to weasels."

"Figures," said Jess.

Matt stopped to get his bearings. "I wonder where we are."

"I know exactly where we are," said Jess: "www.grannysworld.com. You got us here. Now get us out!"

"I'm working on it," said Matt.

They walked along the yellow plastic road, looking for an exit. Jess began having an uneasy feeling that there might not be one. In that case they were in serious trouble, because so far nothing about Granny Goose's Fun Farm was fun. Susie Sunflower spit at them. Sassy Seagull unloaded on them. And Harvey Hamster was anything but happy when Jess accidentally stepped in his Happy Hole.

"Watch where you put your feet, doofus!" he screamed at her.

"Aren't hamsters related to rats?" Jess asked.

Matt nodded.

They trudged on in gloomy silence, a far cry from Dorothy and her friends skipping off to see the wizard.

They followed the road around the lake. Matt noticed a short, stout figure in a checked suit sitting on a park bench, smoking a cigar and reading a magazine. He was the first creature they had seen so far who didn't look as if he was made of plastic. "Look, Jess!" Matt cried. "That man over there—I think he's an elf. Maybe he knows the way out. Let's ask him."

"Drop it, Matt!" Jess exclaimed. "Don't mess with little people. That's how our last adventure began. You remember what we had to go through to get home."

"But it wasn't Elfric's fault," said Matt. "He's a good guy. The elves were on our side, remember? I'm going to ask for directions. It can't hurt."

"Oh, yes it can!" Jess muttered as she ran to keep up with Matt.

"Hello, Mr. Elf!" Matt began, speaking far more cheerfully than he felt. "We have a friend who's an elf, too. Or he used to be an elf. Now he's a giant. His name's Elfric. We were wondering if you know him."

The little man looked up from his magazine. He took the cigar from his mouth and blew a thin stream of smoke in Matt's direction. "Tough luck, kid. Can't help you. Never heard of the guy. Which isn't surprising. I'm not an elf. I'm a dwarf."

"Sorry," said Matt.

"Don't mention it." The dwarf went back to his magazine, *Buff Bikini Babes*. He turned it sideways to ogle the centerfold.

"Aren't you embarrassed to look at sleazy pictures like that in public?" Jessica asked.

The dwarf glanced up from Miss October. "Why should I be? I *am* Sleazy."

"Well, duh! Like I couldn't have guessed!" It wasn't much of a secret. The dwarf's suit looked as if he slept in it. Grease stains spotted his shirt and tie. He hadn't shaved in a couple of days.

"No, really! *I am Sleazy*. It's my name, get it?"

"Why would you want a name like that?" Matt asked.

"Grumpy's better? Sneezy? How'd you like to go through life as Dopey? Mom and Pop weren't the sharpest knives in the drawer when it came to naming their kids. You probably heard of my seven brothers. They were in a movie: *Snow White and the Seven Dwarfs*. I missed my chance to go to Hollywood. I'd already left home by then."

"Why?" asked Jessica.

"You ever work in a mine? Try it sometime. You won't be singing 'Hi-ho! Hi-ho!' I guarantee it."

Matt cut in. "Sorry we bothered you, Mr. Sleazy. We really hope you'll help us. You see, we're lost. We need to find the exit. Can you point us in the right direction?"

"You don't like the Fun Farm? Awww! How am I going to break the news to Granny Goose?" Sleazy pointed to an oak tree with his cigar. "Go knock on that oak. Tell Nutsy that Sleazy sent you. He'll handle everything."

"Thanks!"

"See you around." Sleazy stuck the cigar in his mouth and returned to his magazine.

Matt and Jess walked over to the oak. Jess

knocked on the trunk three times. A squirrel stuck his head out of a hole.

"Whaddya want? Spit it out! Don't take all day! If you make me miss *Roller Derby,* I'm gonna be mad."

"Are you Nutsy?" Jessica asked.

"Yeah! What's it to you?"

"Chill, Nutsy! This will only take a minute. You'll be back cheering for the Boston Bombers in no time," Jessica said. "Here's the deal. We want to exit this website. Sleazy sent us. He said you'll handle everything."

"You're Sleazy's pals? Okay, give me a second."

The squirrel disappeared back into the hole. Jessica whispered to Matt, "I can't believe I'm having a conversation with a squirrel. This is getting weird."

"I have the feeling it's going to get weirder," Matt replied. Just then the squirrel came back.

"You want to leave? Where do you want to go?"

"Home," Jessica told him.

"Right away? Or maybe you want to have some fun? As long as you're here . . ."

"What kind of fun?" Matt asked.

"Ever been to a rock concert?"

"Cool!" said Jess. "Who's playing?"

"You'll find out," said Nutsy. He pulled on a twig. The ground beneath Matt and Jess's feet opened, shooting them down a long, dark tunnel.

"This is the last time I trust a squirrel!" Jessica shouted as she sped along.

"Yeah!" Matt agreed. "Especially one named Nutsy!"

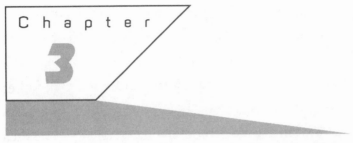

Rock On!

Thump! Jess and Matt opened their eyes and looked around. They had come through a heating duct at the top of a high concrete wall. Fortunately, they landed on a six-foot stack of gym mats, so no bones were broken.

Jess looked around at the bare concrete walls. "Where are we? Why did I let that stupid squirrel talk me into going to a rock concert? We could have been home by now."

Matt agreed. "We'll just have to find another way out. What is this place? It smells like a gym. Uh-oh! I hope we're not in school. Is somebody going to make us do P.E.? I didn't bring a gym suit."

"Don't panic," said Jess, sliding down from the mats to the ground. "This place is way too big for a school gym. Look at all the stuff in here! Goalposts, ice hockey nets, boxing ring. It's more like a storeroom for a sports arena."

"Yeah," Matt said, sliding down to join her. "I wonder if we can get free tickets to something."

Suddenly the walls began shaking.

"I'll settle for a ticket out!" Jess yelled. Matt couldn't hear her. She could hardly hear herself. A solid wall of sound burst open the double doors. It swept over them like an invisible tidal wave, knocking Jess and Matt to the floor and rolling them around like pebbles on the beach.

"What was that?" Jess groaned as the noise dropped down to a deep, rumbling growl.

"B-flat," Matt said, taking his fingers out of his ears. "Someone's trying to tune a bass. There must be a band practicing next door."

"They need a lot of practice," Jess replied, shaking her head to clear her ears. "Let's check this out." They peeked out the double doors into the depths of the darkened arena.

"Nutsy was right. It *is* a rock concert! There must be ten thousand people out there!" Matt exclaimed.

"Twenty thousand!" said Jess. They slipped out the door and joined the crowd milling around under the stage. "I wonder who's playing?" she asked Matt.

"Not 'N Sync," said Matt. That was definitely a no-brainer. The people in the audience looked like the cast from a crowd scene in a Bible movie, except that it would be hard to tell which Bible story they were filming. Some, in flowing robes, backpacks, and headcloths, looked like Israelites about to leave Egypt. Others in chains and black leather looked as if they were waiting for the next chariot race. Then there were those who looked like a tour group from Sodom and Gomorrah. They hardly wore anything to show off their tattoos. What wasn't tattooed was pierced.

"Look at that guy's nose ring! He looks like the blue ribbon bull at the State Fair," Jess whispered to Matt.

"Look at the girl next to him," Matt whispered back. "I think she pierced her head!"

"Cool!" they both said together. A blond Gothic

guy handed them a bag of pretzels. A tattooed lattice of Vikings battling dragons covered his arms from shoulders to wrists. "Take all you want," he offered.

"Gee, thanks!" said Jess, helping herself to a handful. She passed the bag to Matt.

"Want me to pierce your tongue?" the guy's girlfriend asked, taking a four-inch spike out of her lower lip.

"Not really," Jess and Matt replied. "Wouldn't that hurt?"

The girl laughed. "Naaah! It's beyond pain!"

"Then why do it?"

"We're making a statement," her boyfriend answered.

"What is it?" Jess asked.

The Goths raised their fists. Together they shouted, "Just say no!"

"No to what?"

"To being normal!"

"We're getting the message," Matt answered.

"This must be like Woodstock," Jess whispered.

"What's that?" Matt asked.

"It was some rock concert a long, long time ago," Jess explained. "Like in the Dark Ages. Grandpa always talks about it when we're watching MTV. He fell in the mud, broke his leg, didn't eat or drink for three days, lost his car, got arrested."

"Sweet! Sounds like a real good time," said Matt. "Is that like when they had all those guys with guitars and long hair singing about love and peace?"

"Yeah."

"I hope this concert isn't going to be like that."

"Me, too!" said Jess. "BO-RING!"

The crowd began to stir. People held up flashlights, matches, glow sticks, cigarette lighters. Everyone began chanting:

"No Fairy Tales! No Fairy Tales!"

"What's wrong with fairy tales?" Jess asked the Goths.

"Nothing! That's the band's name," the guy with the Viking tattoos explained. "Red's on drums, Beauty's on bass, Cindi plays lead, and Punzi backs her on keyboard. Snow does vocals. Wait till you see her! The babe rocks!"

"What did he say?" Matt asked above the roar of the chanting.

"Beats me," Jess answered. "I think it's a girl group. Like the Spice Girls."

She couldn't have been more wrong.

The stage lights came on. The crowd started screaming:

"Snow! Snow! Snow! Snow! Snow! Snow!"

Five young women tore across the stage in an explosion of black leather, vinyl, and neon. They grabbed their instruments and hacked into their first number like Paul Bunyan felling a tree with a chain saw. The singer snarled at the crowd. Her spiked and dyed blonde hair and corpse-white complexion clashed with a red and green miniskirt decorated with snowflakes and a shredded motorcycle jacket held together with studs and safety pins. She stomped around the stage in thick-soled Doc Martens boots, screaming into the microphone:

"Kill the dwarfs! Kill the dwarfs!
Kill the dwarfs! Kill the dwarfs!"

"Snow! We love you! You're fantastic!" the Goths hollered.

"Drop dead!" she screamed back at them.

"What does she have against dwarfs?" Jess asked.

Matt shook his head. "Can't hear you!"

And no wonder! Power chords made the concrete floor vibrate. The people in front of the stage began jumping up and down, slamming into each other. "Mosh! Mosh!" someone started yelling. The Goth guy picked Jessica up and passed her over his head into the crowd.

"Put me down!" Jess yelled. But no one heard her, for by now the singer had abandoned the lyrics and lay rolling around on the stage, screaming her lungs out. The guitarists started smashing up their instruments.

"We're crowd-surfing!" said Matt as he passed Jessica on his way to the opposite side of the mosh pit.

"We'll never get out alive!" Jess wailed. The singer threw aside the mike, then dived off the lip of the stage. Fights broke out. Two guys began punching each other. Four girls began punching the guys. Suddenly the arena lights came on. Security guards appeared at the exits. A voice came over the sound system, saying, "The concert is over. Please walk

quietly to the exits." A recording of Elton John singing "Crocodile Rock" followed.

"Drop dead!" everybody yelled, and rushed the security guards.

"Matt!" Jess screamed.

"Here I am!" Matt grabbed Jess's hand. They ran frantically back and forth, looking for a way out of the riot.

"Hey, kids! Over here!" Someone waved to them from behind the ruins of a concession stand.

"It's that dwarf, Sleazy!" Jess shouted. She and Matt pushed their way toward him.

"What's the matter, kids? Had enough rock 'n' roll?" Sleazy tapped the ash off his cigar.

"Very funny!" said Jess. "You and your squirrelly pal Nutsy got us into this. Now get us out!"

"No problem! Follow me." Sleazy took a ring of keys out of his pocket. He unlocked a door labeled SECURITY. Jess and Matt followed him through twisting concrete tunnels into the bowels of the arena. They encountered several other locked doors along the way, but Sleazy had keys to all of them. He unlocked the final door. It opened onto a parking lot. Matt and Jess heard police sirens in the distance.

"Uh-oh! The cops are on their way! I'd get out of here fast if I were you!" Sleazy said.

Jessica started shouting. "Where are we gonna go? We don't even know where we are! Come on, Sleazy! We want to go home."

"You promised to help us!" Matt said.

"Don't worry, kid. Sleazy never lets his pals down." The dwarf took another key ring out of his pocket and handed it to Matt. "You'll need wheels to get where you want to go. Go to the end of the row. It's parked in the last space. You can't miss it. Turn right when you leave the lot. Keep going straight till you hit the freeway, then follow the signs. You'll know what to do."

"But . . . we don't know how to drive! We don't have licenses . . . or insurance!" Jess stammered.

Sleazy tapped his cigar. "When did that ever stop anybody?"

"Let's go!" said Matt. "We'll figure it out later." The police sirens were getting louder.

"*Hasta la vista, amigos!*" Sleazy called as Matt and Jess ran down the row of parked vehicles.

"Your mom was right," Matt said. "This is turning into a really exciting game. We got to go to a rock concert, and now we're going to get our own car. I wonder what it's going to be. What kind of car do you think a guy like Sleazy drives? 'Vette? Beamer? SUV? Jag?"

"Try Tacomobile," said Jess.

They saw it standing beneath the parking lot floodlights—a giant taco on wheels, decked out with lettuce, cheese, refried beans, shredded chicken, and guacamole.

"I guess this *is* a multicultural game," Matt stammered. "Did you hear how Sleazy spoke Spanish to us?"

"Crabcakes! He's just cheap!" Jess pointed to the used-car sticker on the windshield. "Look at that! Twenty-eight dollars for a car!"

"It's a lot for a taco," said Matt. "Even with extra beef and cheese."

Jess opened the door in the taco shell, trying not to get guacamole on her hands. "If you like it, then you can drive."

"Deal!" Matt said.

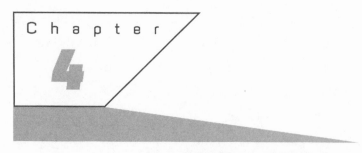

Endless Highway

"Bad driving beats good walking," said Matt as he drove the Tacomobile out of the parking lot. He made a right turn onto the street, past the police cars streaking toward the stadium with sirens screaming. Matt had never driven a real car, but in computer games he and Jess had powered all kinds of vehicles. Making the adjustment wasn't difficult.

Matt turned on the wipers to clear away the sour cream and guacamole dripping onto the windshield. Jess hunched down in her seat. "I don't want anyone to see me," she muttered.

"What's the big deal?" said Matt. "We're not going to run into anyone we know. It's only a computer game. Pretend you're playing a role."

"Yeah," said Jess. "Miss Taco! You like this game, don't you, Matt?"

"It's challenging," Matt replied. "In every other computer adventure we've been on, we knew right from the beginning what the problem was and what we had to do. This game is different. It's like playing pinball, except we're the balls. There's no manual, no help menu, no phone number to call for technical assistance. We're completely on our own. The challenge is to figure out what the problem is and to find the clues that are going to help us solve it. They can be anywhere!"

"So what you're saying is, it's like playing Myst or Riven," said Jess. "No thanks! I've played games like that. It can take months to find some of those clues."

"It won't take us that long," Matt promised. "We have Sleazy to help us if we get stuck."

"I don't trust Sleazy."

"He hasn't let us down yet. You don't like him because he's short."

"No, Matt. I don't like him because he's sleazy."

Up ahead they saw signs for the freeway entrance. "Which way do we go?" Matt asked. "Sleazy told us to follow the signs, but he didn't say which signs to follow."

"See what I mean?" said Jess. "You really can't be sure if Sleazy's helping us or not." She looked at the signs. The one to the right read:

BORING

NOWHERE

DULLSVILLE

The one to the left read:

FUN!

EXCITEMENT!

ADVENTURE!

"Which way?" Matt asked.

"Left!" Jess yelled. Matt hung a hard left. The Tacomobile cruised onto the freeway.

"Hey! This taco has great pick up!" Matt exclaimed as he zoomed past cars and trucks.

"It runs on salsa," Jess pointed out. "Look at the dashboard. There's a chili pepper by the gas gauge."

"And it's turbocharged with beans!" Matt exclaimed. "Indy 500—here we come!"

They drove through the night, taking turns at the wheel. At dawn they stopped at a rest area to wash up and use the bathroom. Jess looked around at the flat landscape. "There's nothing here," she yawned. "I wonder how much longer it's going to take to get to wherever it is we're supposed to be going."

"This sure is boring," Matt agreed. "I wonder if we're going the right way."

"I read the signs. This is the right way, all right. Except that if this is someone's idea of fun, excitement, and adventure, I'd hate see what they call Dullsville."

They climbed back into the Tacomobile. "See if you can find a good station on the radio," Matt asked as he drove back onto the freeway.

"There's good news and bad news," said Jess, alternately pushing buttons and reading from the driver's manual in the glove compartment. "The good news is this Tacomobile comes equipped with more than a radio. It has a TV, CB, CD player, and VCR. It's a total system."

"Cool!" Matt exclaimed.

"The bad news is I can't find a station. Nobody's broadcasting in Gameland. There are no disks or tapes. We're going to have to get by on conversation for the next ten thousand miles."

"It's too bad there aren't any tapes," said Matt. "It would be interesting to see what kind of videos a guy like Sleazy watches."

"I don't think I want to know that," said Jess. "Hey, slow down! There's a hitchhiker up ahead."

Matt squinted through the guacamole streaks coating the windshield. "Look who it is, Jess! It's that singer from the concert last night! How did she get here?" Matt stepped on the brakes. He steered the Tacomobile onto the shoulder at the right side of the road and stopped.

Jess opened the door. "Need a ride?" she hollered.

"Do I! Thanks a million, guys!" The girl grabbed her backpack and came running. Jess slid over to make room as the girl jumped in.

"Hi! I'm Snow. Where are you headed?"

"I'm Jess, and this is my pal, Matt. We don't know where we're going. And don't ask why we're driving this taco. It's a long story."

"Cool!" said Snow. "I don't know where I'm going either. And I love Mexican food."

"We were at your concert last night," Matt said as he steered the Tacomobile back onto the freeway. "You were awesome! Too bad the cops broke it up."

Snow shrugged. "No biggie. It happens all the time. We never get to play for more than five minutes anywhere before there's a riot. Beauty—she's on bass—says that if we don't start a riot, we're not really playing. You gotta have soul, man!" She shook her fist under Jess's nose. "It's gotta come from here!" She thumped the studs and safety pins on her jacket. "Get it?"

"Uh . . . yeah!" said Jess. "I have a question. Why do you hate short people? That's kind of prejudiced, don't you think?"

Snow turned the rearview mirror so that it reflected her face. She smeared a slash of black lipstick across her mouth. Then she began talking and waving her arms around like a videotape played at FAST FORWARD. "I don't hate short people. What a stupid idea! Short people, tall people, thin people, fat people—what does it matter? People are people. People need people. The only people who aren't people are prejudiced people. Prejudiced people are stupid. I hate them all!" She began banging her fists on her forehead, screaming. "Prejudice makes me crazy! Crazy! Crazy! Crazy!"

Matt flashed Jess an "I think we made a big mistake" look. But Jess kept her cool and continued asking questions.

"If that's how you feel about it, why were you singing that song 'Kill the Dwarfs'? What's that supposed to mean?"

"It means what it says. I hate dwarfs. Dwarfs aren't people. They're nasty, sneaky, selfish little jerks. I spent a whole summer vacation as a live-in nanny for seven of them! I cooked. I cleaned. I did laundry. I did everything for those icky little buggers except wipe their nasty behinds. They would have had me do that, too, if they'd thought of it. The creeps! So don't preach to me about dwarfs! I hate

dwarfs! KILL THE DWARFS! AAARRUUGGHH!"
She began beating her head again.

"I think we picked up a clue," said Matt.

"We picked up something," Jess muttered. "I only hope it's not catching."

Matt turned to Snow. "Excuse me, Miss Snow. Sorry for interrupting, but may I ask you a question?"

"Sure!" said Snow, lighting up like a rainbow after a thunderstorm. "What do you want to know?"

"You say you spent the summer working for seven dwarfs. Is your last name . . . White?"

"Uh-huh!"

"And is your mom—I mean your stepmom—in politics?"

"Is she ever! She's the queen, man! And she's wicked!"

"Ohmigosh!" gasped Jess. "Then that means . . ."

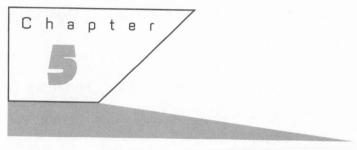

Chapter

5

'Bot Attack

". . . you're the real Snow White! Wow! I never met anyone from a fairy tale before!" Jess exclaimed. "Can I have your autograph?"

"Sure!" said Snow. She fished a pen out of her backpack and scrawled her signature on a crumpled piece of paper. "Come see us at our next concert. I'll get you autographs from the whole band."

"Speaking of the band," Matt began. "Didn't you say your bass player's name was Beauty? Does she take a lot of naps?"

"No," Snow replied. "But her boyfriend's a biker. He has this beard that goes down to his waist."

"Don't tell me!" said Jess. "And everyone calls him The Beast?"

"How'd you guess that?" Snow asked.

Jess shrugged. "Just a hunch. I bet we can figure out the whole band. Who's on lead guitar?"

"Cindi."

"She has extra-tiny feet. Like a size three? Buys her shoes in the kids' department? Am I right?"

"You nailed it!" said Snow. "What about keyboard? I'll give you a hint. We call her Punzi."

"And she has extra-long hair?" suggested Matt.

"Her mom's a real witch," Jess added.

"Right on!" said Snow. "Guess drums, and you can have one of our CDs."

"Let's see . . . I remember that she had red hair. Real red!" said Jess.

"And she was wearing this cloak thing," said Matt.

"LITTLE RED RIDING HOOD!" they both shouted together.

"All right!" Snow applauded. She opened her backpack. "Here are the three CDs we have out right now: *Road Kill Wolf, Poison the Prince,* and *Dwarf Guts.* You're gonna love *Road Kill Wolf.* We recorded it live. Red smashes up her whole drum kit while the rest of us run around the stage, howling and screaming. It's supposed to sound like a fleet of monster trucks running down a wolf pack. It's awesome! Wanna hear it?"

"Not just yet," said Matt. "I still have a question to ask. It sounds like all of you ran away from your fairy tales. Why? Aren't you supposed to live happily ever after?"

Not a good question, Jess thought. She could see storm clouds gathering on Snow's face.

"Why did we run away? I'll tell you why! Because 'happily ever after' doesn't include running through dark, dangerous woods every time your grandma catches cold! 'Happily ever after' is not pounding around on a ballroom floor in tight shoes with a jerk prince stomping on your toes! 'Happily ever after' does not mean spending the rest of your life weeping over a blind fool who was too stupid and too cheap to buy a decent extension ladder! Ha! That may be somebody else's 'happily ever after,' but it sure ain't mine!"

"What is yours?" Jess asked.

"Listen! I wrote this song. It says it all." Snow shoved *Poison the Prince* into the CD player. The Tacomobile's speakers screamed.

> "Kill the dwarfs! Kill the prince!
> Kill the witch! Kill the ogre!
> Kill the giant! Kill the trolls!
> Kill your fairy godmother! Kill the Grimm Brothers!
> No more fairy tales! No more fairy tales!
> We are free! Free! Free! Free! Free! Free!"

Snow punched the STOP button as the song faded into a buzzing groan. "Do you get it now? Do you know what I mean? Do you know what I'm saying? My 'happily ever after' is not making goo-goo eyes at some twerp of a prince. It's being in a band with my best buds, going where we like, doing what we want, and singing what we feel. That's where it's at! The rest is nowhere, man! It isn't even on the charts!"

"If that's so, then how come you're out here all alone, thumbing a ride in the middle of nowhere?" Jess asked. "Where's the rest of your band?"

"We had to split up for a while," Snow said, dropping her eyes and fumbling with her backpack. "Don't ask why. I'd rather not talk about it."

"Okay," said Matt. He looked over at Jess. "Do you know you're getting a zit?"

"Where?"

"On your left cheek. In front of your ear."

Jess looked in the mirror. Sure enough, she saw a red dot. She put her finger over it. The dot appeared on the back of her finger. "That's not a zit," she said to Matt. "It's coming from outside somewhere. It's some kind of laser dot."

Snow thrust her head out the side window. "Aw, no! There they are! How did they track me down?"

"Who? What? Where?" Jess shouted.

"Yo'bots! Turn!" Snow yelled at Matt.

"What are yo'bots?" Matt asked.

"I don't have time to explain. Turn! Turn!"

"How? We're in the middle of a freeway!" Matt hollered.

Snow grabbed the wheel, pulling the Tacomobile into a hard right. Jess screamed. Tires screeched. Cheese and lettuce flew everywhere. Matt covered his eyes as they made a ninety-degree turn on two wheels.

Something the size of a sports car whooshed past. A chunk of freeway exploded in a burst of orange flame. Bits of asphalt rained down as the Tacomobile bounced across the median.

"That will kill the guacamole." Matt sighed.

"That will kill us if you don't floor it!" Snow screamed. Matt put the pedal to the metal, sending the Tacomobile tearing down the freeway in the opposite direction.

"What's happening? Who are those guys? Why are they after us?" Jess demanded to know.

"I told you."

"No, you didn't! What's a yo'bot?"

"A yo'bot is cyborg, an android, a robot that looks human. Except yo'bots have TV sets where their heads should be. They fly yo'pods!"

"Why do you call them yo'bots?"

"Because they dress like rappers, and the TVs are always tuned to rap channels. Get it?"

"Yo!" said Jess.

"They're not the worst," Snow continued. "There

are SWAT'bots, too. They wear camouflage, like SWAT teams, and tune in to Arnold Schwarzenegger movies."

"*Hasta la vista,* baby!" said Matt in a thick German accent.

"It's not funny, man!" said Snow. "Our band has had to dodge them more times than I care to think about. The only reason we've gotten away so far was because they have to break every fifteen minutes for commercials."

"I don't get it," said Jess. "Why would someone want to rub you out? Just because they don't like your music? That's crazy!"

"It's crazy, all right," Snow explained. "But don't think it has anything to do with music. It's about changing the story. There are some people—very powerful people—who don't like the idea of characters coming up with their own endings. Everybody's supposed to follow the script. Don't think. Just do what you're told. Leave everything to Granny. Or else!"

"Or else what? Who's Granny? You mean the old lady in *Little Red Riding Hood*?" Jess asked.

"No! Red's granny can't even figure out how to

use her remote. Red had to run over all the time to change the channels. The granny I'm talking about is . . . never mind. Can't go into it now. The yo'bots are coming around. Turn! TURN!"

Matt hung a hard right. As the Tacomobile swerved, Jess caught a glimpse of half a dozen yellow disks hovering in the sky. They looked like a squadron of flying saucers, except each one had a frowny face painted on its bottom. A mean, angry frowny face that looked as if it were about to say: I don't like you, and I'm gonna do something about it!

Two yo'pods detached themselves from the squadron. Jess saw them in the rearview mirror. A red dot appeared on the dashboard. "Crabcakes!" Jess yelled. "They're targeting us again!"

"What do I do?" Matt yelled.

"Turn! Turn!" Snow shouted.

"Wait!" screamed Jess. "We can't keep zigzagging back and forth. I have a better idea. Keep driving. Go straight. Leave the rest to me."

Jess unbuckled her seat belt. Bracing her feet against the windshield, she pulled the rearview mirror off its mount.

"What did you do that for? Now I can't see what's coming," Matt complained.

"If this doesn't work, you won't want to see what's coming!" Clutching the mirror in her teeth, Jess crawled over Snow. She sat on the headrest of the backseat, facing backward. Planting her feet firmly in the beans, she braced her back against Snow to hold herself steady. Two yo'pods whirred overhead, three car lengths behind. Jess could see the frowny faces even more clearly now. They had fangs!

A red dot appeared in the middle of Jess's T-shirt. The yo'pods were targeting their missiles right at her. Jessica didn't flinch. She held the mirror steady, reflecting the laser beam up toward the nearest yo'pod so that the red dot was centered on the frowny face's nose.

Matt looked back to see what she was doing. "Is this gonna work?"

"We'll find out in a couple of seconds."

The first yo'pod fired a missile. It came streaking toward Jess, close enough for her to read the letters on its nose cone: GGUS.

"Gee-Gus? I wonder what that means." Jess

watched the missile bank and begin a turn, following the red dot right back to the yo'pod.

Kabloom! The yo'pod flew to bits. Fragments of wreckage struck the second yo'pod. It shuddered in midair, then spun out of control. Jess saw it streak across the freeway. *Kablam!*

"Two down! Way to go!" yelled Snow as the remaining saucers took up the pursuit.

"Faster, Matt!" cried Jess.

"I can't go any faster. We're over two hundred now! We can't keep this up much longer. We're running low on gas . . . I mean, salsa!"

"I know what to do!" said Jess. "There's an exit coming up. Turn off here."

"They're gonna follow us!"

"Let 'em! They won't shoot, now that I know how to deflect their missiles. We have to refill our tank. Otherwise we're roadkill."

"Okay! Hold on!"

Matt spun off the freeway and up the exit ramp, tires screaming, rubber burning, cheese and lettuce flying all the way. They stopped at the light, then turned right onto a wide avenue offering mile after mile of cheap motels, greasy fast-food joints, shabby discount outlets, shady used-car lots, tacky neon signs.

"Gross! This reminds me of a song I wrote," said Snow. " 'Crud Avenue.' Wanna hear it?"

"Not now," said Jess. "Turn right," she told Matt.

Matt turned into the parking lot. He looked up at the flashing sign.

EL SOMBRERO

RESTAURANT & SERVICE STATION

EAT HERE AND GET GAS

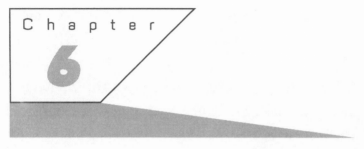

Hot Sauce

Matt and Snow followed Jess into the restaurant. A big rottweiler wearing a beret stood behind the counter. He greeted them in Spanish. *"Hola! ¿Como están, amigos?"*

"Woof! Woof!" Snow remarked. "Who let the dogs out?"

"Buenos días, Señor Perro!" said Matt.

"I don't believe this," said Jess. "This game's multicultural *and* multi-species. Now you're talking to a dog! In Spanish!"

"We've talked to a squirrel. What's the difference?" said Matt. "It's part of the game."

"Okay, but I still think it's weird." Jess flashed a smile at the rottweiler. "*Buenos días, Señor Poochy!* Shouldn't you be a chihuahua?"

"The name's Spike, not Poochy. The chihuahua called in sick. I'm filling in for him. He must've eaten some bad beans. Pizarro's revenge. Haw, haw, haw!" His laughter sounded like panting.

"Don't you mean Montezuma?" Matt asked.

Spike wiped the counter. "Whatever! I was never too good in history. They don't teach that in doggy school. Haw, haw! What'll you have? We got a special today. A dollar off on our new feature: cruditos."

"What's a crudito?" Jess asked.

"It's a burrito with all the extras."

"Extra what?"

"Extra cholesterol, extra calories, extra grease, extra gas. Haw, haw, haw!"

Jess made a face. If she was hungry before, she wasn't now. "Look, Spike, we didn't really come in for something to eat. This is kind of a strange request. Do you have any salsa?"

"Do we have salsa? Does McDonald's have ketchup? Sure we have salsa! There's a whole bin of those little plastic containers by the napkins. How many do you need?"

"About fifty gallons total," Jess told him.

"Give it up!" Spike threw up his paws. "I don't have nearly that much. You'll clean us out. We're not getting a delivery till Friday."

"We can't wait that long," said Matt.

"Uh-oh! Check what just walked in," Snow whispered.

Jess and Matt both turned in time to see eight yo'bots enter the restaurant in double file. They could have been stamped from a mold. Each wore the exact same baggy white jeans and lugs. Thick gold chains festooned with $ signs hung around their necks. Their shirts were all ten sizes too big, with the same PHAT logo. They reeked of Tommy cologne. They talked on identical cell phones.

"They're watching us," Snow told Jess and Matt. "Pretend we don't see them."

The yo'bots sat down at two tables on either side of the door. They slouched on the benches in exactly the same way. They pretended to read six identical copies of *Rapp-It-Upp* magazine. The same Puff Daddy video flickered across their hi-density faces.

"Look who just walked in—Bow-wow-wow!" said Spike.

"Not exactly," Snow murmured. "These aren't cute little kids."

"Oh, man! They look programmed, like VCRs," Matt said.

"They are," Snow replied. "Programmed to track us down and bring us in. Get ready. We may have to run for it."

"How?" said Matt. "If we can't get enough salsa to gas up the Tacomobile, we won't get far."

"Leave it to me," Snow said. "When you're in a band, you learn how to deal with all kinds of critters." She took a ten-dollar bill from her backpack and pushed it across the counter toward the rottweiler. "You make chili here, Spike. Tell me, what's the hottest sauce you have?"

"This stuff," Spike said, placing a bottle of Boca de Fuego hot sauce on the counter. Flames leaped around the letters on the label. "Don't fool around with it. It's dangerous. We use two drops per hundred gallons."

"Whoa!" Jess and Matt exclaimed.

"Cool! Just what we need." Snow slipped the

bottle into her backpack. "Now do you have a rear entrance somewhere? We're trying to lose those dudes." She cocked her head toward the door.

"I dig it!" Spike gave Snow a wink. "Go past the rest rooms. You can't miss it."

Snow whispered to Matt and Jess. "Okay, guys, here's how we're gonna do this. We'll leave one at a time. Matt, you go first. Pretend like nothing's happening, like you're just going to use the rest room. Get the Tacomobile started and wait. Jess, you're next. Open the salsa tank before you get in with Matt. Count to one hundred. If I'm not out by then, take off. Don't worry about the yo'bots. They won't come after you. I'm the one they want."

"Why?" Matt asked.

"I'll tell you later. There isn't time now. Go!" Snow said.

Matt strolled toward the rest room. He paused before the door marked with a bull, a cactus, and the word SEÑORES to make sure no one was watching. Then he opened the other door marked EMPLOYEES ONLY and slipped outside. Matt dashed across the parking lot to the Tacomobile. He slid into the driver's seat. At the same time, he popped the little door in the taco shell covering the salsa tank.

He had just started the engine when he saw Jess coming. She slipped in from the other side.

"Did you unscrew the salsa cap?" Matt asked.

"Yeah!" said Jess. "Everything's set. Now we count to a hundred. I sure hope Snow's okay."

"So do I!" said Matt, nervously, moving the automatic gearshift between Park and Drive. "One . . . two . . . three . . ."

They had counted to eighty-six when Snow came running. She burst out the rear door with eight yo'bots hot on her heels.

"Get going!" Jess screeched. Matt shoved the gearshift into Reverse as Snow piled in. "I didn't have time to use the eyedropper. I dumped in the whole bottle." Yo'bots surrounded the Tacomobile, climbing on the shell. Jess found herself staring Eminem in the face. Snoop Dogg stood on the cheese, glowering at Snow and Matt.

"I don't know. This chili sauce doesn't seem to be doing anything," said Matt, turning around to back out. Suddenly the tachometer needle spun around the dial. Sheets of flame poured out of the exhaust.

The Tacomobile shot across the parking lot, scattering yo'bots and crushing yo'pods like tin cans.

"I didn't mean to do that," said Matt. "Can we get sued?"

"Who cares! Gun it!" Jess shouted.

Matt slammed the gearshift into Drive and stomped the accelerator. The Tacomobile screamed toward the exit. They were airborne by the time they reached the curb.

"How fast are we going?" Jess asked.

"I don't know," Matt told her. "The speedometer blew out."

Snow glanced out the window. "Look, guys! We're past the moon." The vast lunar surface filled the window. Within seconds, it began receding into the distance, replaced by an enormous red sphere.

"You better slow down, Matt!" said Jess. "I think that's Mars coming up."

"I can't!" Matt wailed. "The brakes don't work. We're picking up speed!"

"This is like *Star Trek*!" said Jess.

"More like *Lost in Space*," Snow added as the Red Planet shot by. "Spike the Rottweiler wasn't kidding. Man, that was some powerful chili sauce!

Look! The stars are blinking out. We must be going faster than light speed. Awesome!"

"EEEEEEEEEE!" Jess and Matt squealed as the Tacomobile swooped past the moons of Pluto, racing toward the outer limits of deepest, darkest space.

Space Cadets

The Tacomobile drifted on the solar wind. Bits of lettuce, chunks of grated cheese, and clumps of sour cream and guacamole revolved around it like the satellite moons of an undiscovered planet.

Matt stomped the accelerator. "Any luck?" Snow asked.

Matt shook his head. "Nothing. We're dead in the cosmos. We're out of gas, salsa, chili sauce. You name it, we ain't got it."

"Well, isn't that a hoot!" Jess snapped. "I said, 'I don't like this game. I don't want to play it.' You said, 'Play it! What's the harm? You'll figure it out and be done in five minutes.' Five minutes, you said! So here we are, hours later, floating in outer space somewhere beyond the Milky Way. We don't know where we are. We don't know where we're going. We don't know how to get home. We don't know what we're supposed to do. We're clueless! We don't even know what galaxy we're in. Okay, Mr. Wizard! You got us into this. Now figure a way to get us out!"

"I'm working on it," said Matt, fiddling with the channel selector buttons on the TV-VCR set.

"Chill, Jess!" said Snow. "Just sit back and enjoy the ride. Plenty of people would pay a lot of money for a view like this. It inspired me to write a song. I'm calling it 'Window on the Galaxy.' Wanna hear it?" Snow closed her eyes, banged her fists against her head, and started screeching:

> "Looking out my window.
> I see the universe
> I see Andromeda
> I see the Crab Nebula
> I see the Horsehead Nebula . . ."

Jess rolled her eyes. "Crabcakes! If I ever get home again, I swear I'm giving up computer games. I'll learn creative cross-stitch. I'll have Grandma teach me knitting. . . ."

"Hold it! I'm getting a signal!" Matt cried. The onboard TV screen flickered. Familiar images came into view. Familiar words cut through the speaker static: "Here's the story . . . of a man named Grady . . ."

"I don't believe it," said Jess. "We're picking up *The Grady Bunch* in outer space?"

"Who are the Gradys? I don't watch TV much," Snow asked.

"They're kind of like dwarfs, only they're cute. And there are more of them," Matt explained.

"Dwarfs!? I hate dwarfs! Wanna know what I think of dwarfs?"

"Never mind. We already know," said Jess.

"It is a real signal; it's not just random space static. And it's coming from that star!" Matt pointed straight ahead.

"We're moving!" said Jess. "Look, Matt! The numbers on the odometer are turning."

They were—faster and faster, until the digital display dissolved into a cloudy blur. The distant star grew brighter as they approached. Its vastness filled the windshield.

"What in the galaxy is that?" Matt gasped. "It looks like Saturn!"

"It even has rings," Jess added.

The patterns on the rings formed letters as the Tacomobile approached:

UNIVERSE STUDIOS! . . . WHERE STARS ARE BORN! . . . HITMAKER TO THE GALAXY! . . . BRINGING YOU TOMORROW'S SHOWS TODAY!

"Advertising!" Snow shrieked. "I don't believe this! Somebody stuck ugly billboards out in space!"

"It's not just a billboard. There are videos, too," Matt observed.

Images revolved around the rings like an electronic sign in a mall. Giant photos of Marilyn Monroe, Princess Diana, Madonna, Elvis, Queen Elizabeth, swimsuit models, movie stars, TV stars, tennis players, wrestlers, cuddly babies, cowboys, soldiers, and homeless people chased one another around the planet's circles like hamsters on a wheel. The images changed back to words.

WELCOME TO UNIVERSE STUDIO'S FAMILY FUN TOUR . . . OUR DIRECTIONAL BEAM HAS TAKEN CONTROL OF YOUR VEHICLE AND WILL GUIDE YOU TO YOUR PERSONAL PARKING SPACE IN THE PARKING KINGDOM. . . . OUR CHEERFUL GUIDES ARE WAITING TO GREET YOU. . . . WHILE PREPARING TO DOCK, PLEASE SET YOUR RECEIVER TO **999.000** TO ENJOY OUR PROGRAM OF SOOTHING SOUNDS AND VIDEOS.

"Let's check it out!" Jess punched the numbers into the receiver. The Gradys disappeared, replaced by a rap group in living color.

"Yo! I need TV! Yo! You need TV! We need TV! See!
TV for you! TV for me!
No trouble! No pain!
Watch TV! Turn off yo' brain!"

A chorus of barely dressed young women wiggled their hips, crooning into microphones, "Teevee . . . teevee . . . teevee . . ."

"This is making me sleepy," said Jess.

"This makes me want to watch more TV," said Matt.

Snow stared at the screen. "I know that guy! It's 8-Trak! He writes incredible poetry. He used to be a revolutionary. Why is he singing about watching TV? Where did those hootchie-cootchie girls come from? What's going on?"

"I think 8-Trak sold out," said Matt.

"Yeah," Jess added. "8-Trak went digital."

"This isn't funny, guys! It's scary. Real scary!" Before Snow finished, the rappers disappeared. A spectacularly beautiful teenage girl replaced them on the screen. She had beautiful hair, beautiful skin, beautiful eyes, beautiful teeth, beautiful clothes, and a beautiful figure. She spoke with a beautiful voice.

"Hi! I'm Tiffany. I have lots of friends. They all say I look like a fairy-tale princess. And my life is a fairy tale. I love being me, because I'm beautiful. I'm popular. And, what's most important, I'm normal. Are you beautiful, like me? Are you popular? No? Well, maybe that's because . . ." Tiffany glared from the screen. "YOU'RE NOT NORMAL! And if you're not normal . . . YOU'RE NEVER GOING TO HAVE A DATE! YOU'RE NEVER GOING

TO HAVE A BOYFRIEND! EVERYBODY WILL HATE YOU AND LAUGH AT YOU! AND YOU'LL PROBABLY DIE, OLD AND ALONE, IN A CRUMMY ROOM IN SOME FLEABAG MOTEL! But don't worry . . ." Tiffany smiled her warm, beautiful smile. "Because if you watch TV hour after hour, day after day, like I do, you'll learn what to wear, what to eat, what to say, and what to think so that you'll be normal, too! Then you can be beautiful and popular and everyone will love you. Then you'll be happy. Like me!"

Tiffany twinkled on and on about her beautifully styled hair and makeup. Snow groaned. "Man! Where did they find her? Is she for real? Who does she think she's kidding?"

Jess and Matt made no response. Their eyes focused straight ahead at the receiver screen as they chanted, "Popular . . . normal . . . beautiful . . . TV is good. . . . TV is our friend. . . . We love TV. . . ."

"Guys! Snap out of it, guys! Can't you see what's going on? You're being brainwashed! Don't you understand? This is the whole 'Fairy-Tale Princess Lives Happily Ever After' trip! This is what I ran away from! This is why I had to escape from my stepmother, from the dwarfs, from the prince! I know girls like Tiffany. They wear enough makeup to plaster a wall. They can't eat a meal without throwing up. They have no personality, no self-respect. If that's normal, we don't want any part of it!"

Jess and Matt paid no attention. They stared through Snow, as if she weren't there. "TV is good. TV makes us happy. . . . TV is our friend. . . ."

"Omigosh! They're totally brainwashed! Some alien force must be controlling their minds." Snow reached for the OFF button.

"I saw that! Don't try to turn me off, Miss White!" Tiffany snapped. "That's right! I know who you are. Maybe you don't want to marry Prince Charming, but I do! Keep your hands off the receiver. We control the reception now. What you see, what you feel, what you think—we decide!"

"I've heard of interactive TV, but this is ridiculous," Snow said. "Okay, Tiff. I see you know all the answers. Have it your way. Here are my hands. I'm holding them up so you can see them."

"That's better," Tiffany said. "Don't ever interfere with our programming selections again."

"I won't! Believe me, I learned my lesson," Snow replied as Jess and Matt chanted on. "Uh, excuse me, Tiffany. Were you planning on going out tonight? To the ball, maybe? Prince Charming will be there? You're going to wear the glass slippers and the new liquid Miracle Bra you bought at Victoria's Secret? Well, I hate to tell you this, but I think you're getting a zit on your forehead."

Tiffany turned pale beneath her makeup. "A ZIT! I CAN'T HAVE ZITS! THE BALL IS TONIGHT! I'VE BOOKED THE COACH! I'VE RENTED THE PUMPKIN! I CAN'T LET THE PRINCE SEE ME LIKE THIS! WHAT AM I GOING TO DO?"

"I don't know, but you better do something. And fast," said Snow. "That's a real headlight you're growing. I'll bet it's visible from the next galaxy. The astronomers there are probably tracking it now. They'll think they discovered a supernova."

"EEEEEEEEEEE!" Tiffany ran off in tears.

"What a wimp! She's worse than Cindi's stepsisters. And now it's time for a station break." Snow pressed the POWER button. The screen turned black.

"TV is cool. . . . TV makes us popular. . . . TV is . . ." The chanting stopped. Jess rubbed her eyes.

Matt blinked rapidly, as if waking from a deep sleep. "Where are we? What's going on?" they asked.

"You were hypnotized," Snow explained. "Whoever runs this studio planet tried to use that channel to control your brains."

"It didn't work with you. How come?" Jess wanted to know.

"I'm not sure. I may have more resistance. I don't watch much TV when I'm on the road with the band."

"Uh-oh! We're in trouble," Jess and Matt said at once.

"Not if we work together," Snow assured them. "Just because something's on TV doesn't mean you have to watch it."

Matt looked out the window. "Easier said than done!" The planet's surface loomed into view. It consisted of millions of TV screens, as if every TV set that ever existed had been brought here and turned on. There were big-screen TVs, tiny portables, ancient black-and-whites. It was the Elephants' Graveyard of TVs. And TV shows.

"Why is that man wearing a dress?" Matt wanted to know.

"I think his name is Milton Berle," said Jess. "My grandma told me he was a big star back in the Stone Age. Look! There's Lucy! And Jackie Gleason! I watch them on Nick at Nite!"

The Tacomobile circled in for a landing. The TV portal opened. The Tacomobile followed the control beam inside. It cruised through an inner space lit with shows that no one could recognize.

"I guess these are shows that never made it," Matt suggested.

"Just as well," said Jess. "Who would watch something called *My Mother the Car?*"

The Tacomobile touched down with a bump in the parking area. Looking out, Jess saw acres and acres of vehicles of every description. Trucks, RVs, Mars probes, lunar modules, and flying saucers that could only have come from somewhere beyond the known galaxies filled every space.

"This looks like the lot at Home Depot," said Matt.

"I wonder if we can get a hot dog," Jess remarked.

"How about a taco?" Matt asked.

"Forget it!"

The Tacomobile's doors opened. The images on the screens suddenly changed. Instead of millions of single pictures, each set became a pixel making one giant image that filled the inner space like a thunderhead filling the sky. It was the image of a kindly old lady in a calico dress, wearing her hair in a white bun.

"Hello, Matt and Jess. Hello, Miss White. Welcome to Universe Studios. I've been waiting for you."

Snow gasped. "Granny Goose!"

"Granny Goose! Universe Studios! G-Gus! I saw those letters on the missile when the yo'bots attacked us on the freeway," Jessica cried. "All the clues are falling into place, Matt. It's her! Granny's the one who created the game, who programmed the yo'bots and sent them to capture us!"

"That's right, you little twerp! It took you long enough to figure out."

Granny Goose laughed, a sour, evil laugh that oozed from thousands of TV sets like stale commercials. "I've got you now, Miss Snow White. All of you! You and the rest of your band fell right into my trap! I had my eyes on you every step of the

way, right from the very beginning. Did you really think you could escape? That you could outsmart me?"

"Well, we sure tried," said Snow.

"Too bad you won't get another chance."

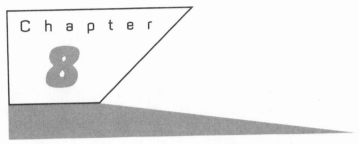

The Cookie Jar

"Busted!" cried Matt and Jess.

"No way!" said Snow. "Here's where I bail!" She hopped out the door and began running across the parking lot.

**Go ahead! You can run, but you can't hide.
Hahahahahahahahahaha!!!!!!!!!**

Granny Goose's voice echoed through the vast space. Snow's face suddenly appeared on every screen.

Snow White! Snow White!
Not too pretty and not too bright!

Snow's own face and own voice taunted her as millions of multiple images congealed into one giant composite Snow.

Granny knows everything about you!
Nobody can run from Granny!

Snow tried. She ran back and forth across the parking lot, confronting her own image everywhere she turned, while her own voice screeched out her most shameful secrets.

"You pig out on pork rinds and chocolate chip cookies when you think no one is looking! You lifted the purple passion lipstick from your best friend Cindi's purse! You went to a rave at the Dwarf Club with Rumpelstiltskin! Yuck! Did you really fall for his 'straw into gold' routine? He's been using that line since the Dark Ages! Loved the black wig! What a clever disguise! Was that really you—duh?!"

Snow collapsed in a sobbing heap. "No more! Please! I can't stand it!"

Granny Goose's face filled the screens. "I know plenty more, honeybunch. This is just the beginning. So any time you'd like me to share what I know about you with all your friends, with the whole universe—"

"No, no!" Snow wailed.

"I thought so. We'll have no more nonsense from you. Don't ever think you can fool Granny Goose! Granny knows everything, so from now on you're going to do whatever Granny says. Take her away." A nearby SWAT'pod flicked on its headlights. The doors opened. A pair of SWAT'bots in helmets and camouflage gear stepped out. They picked Snow up, tossed her inside, and cruised to the far end of the parking lot. The wall of TV screens opened. The pod glided in. The wall closed behind it, as if it never existed.

"Where are they taking Snow?" Jess demanded.

"None of your beeswax!" Granny Goose replied.

"How'd you know all that stuff about her?" Matt asked.

"Granny likes to bake cookies for her little friends," the giant image sneered. "Chocolate chip, walnut raisin. All different kinds of flavors for all different kinds of tastes. And all different kinds of programs. Netscape, Explorer . . ."

"Huh?" said Jess.

"Wait! I get it!" said Matt. "I know the kind of cookies she's talking about! They're little programs someone sneaks into your computer. They let other people keep track of where you go on the Internet. The websites you visit, the products you buy, the e-mail you send. It's like having a spy planted inside your brain."

"But you can delete them," said Jess. "I always get this little message that tells me when someone wants to insert a cookie. There's a whole cookie file in my system folder that I delete, to make sure . . . when I remember."

"That's the point," said Matt. "When you remember. How many people even know about cookies? And what about doughnuts, Ring-Dings, Ho-Hos, and all other kinds of stealth programs that we don't even know are there? They're in our computers or on another database, humming along, collecting all kinds of information about us. And we don't know they exist! It's a big problem!"

"That's right, sugar plum. It is a big problem . . . for you! Not for me! And speaking of websites and databases, did Britney ever answer your e-mail?"

"What!?" Matt squealed. "Britney who? I don't know what you're talking about!"

"Oh, yes you do, kiddo! Why are you turning red? You wrote a love e-mail to Britney Spears. That was sweet of you, Matt, telling her that you thought she was a whole lot prettier than Christina Aguilera. And maybe the two of you could get together the next time she came to town for a concert? In your dreams, baby!"

"Matt! You have a crush on Britney Spears? You actually sent her a love e-mail?" Jess began to giggle. **"Dear Britney, I love you. Please say that you love me."**

Matt looked as if he wanted to crawl into one of the cracks in the floor and disappear. "It was meant as a joke," he mumbled.

"Sure!"

"How about you, sweetie?" Granny Goose said

to Jess. "Maybe Matt wants to know about some of the places you've been visiting. It's only fair."

"No!" Jess snapped.

"Yeah," said Matt. "I want to hear."

"Later, snookums. Granny has other matters that she wants to discuss with you two. In person! I'll see you both in my office. Take the transporter. I'll be waiting for you. With milk and cookies. Don't keep Granny waiting."

The screens went blank.

"We're in trouble. Big trouble," Matt muttered as he began following the signs toward the transporters.

"Britney Spears? What a hoot! So who else have you written to? Christina? Mariah? Oprah?"

"Aw, put a lid on it, Jess! You better not tell anybody!"

"I won't. We both have more important things to think about. You have to hand it to Granny Goose, Matt. She is one sharp cookie, inside or outside of a computer. This game is turning into a real challenge."

"Any ideas about what we do next?" Matt asked. "Granny holds all the cards. And all the cookies."

"I'm working on it," Jess replied.

By now they had reached the transporters. The conveyer modules rode inside clear plastic cylinders that extended up through the ceiling and down through the floor. Matt pushed the **<Enter>** button. The door opened. Matt and Jess stepped inside. A touchpad and viewscreen filled the opposite wall. A menu appeared as the door closed behind them. Matt reached up to tap **<Granny's Office>**.

"Hold on!" said Jess. "Why are you doing that?"

"Granny told us to come to her office."

"So what? Why do we have to do what Granny wants? She can cool her buns. We'll see her when we're good and ready." Jess studied the menu. "Very interesting. Let's check this out." Jess pressed the square labeled **<Studio Tour>**.

"Why are we going on a tour?" Matt protested as the transporter whirred into motion. "Snow's in trouble. Granny's on our case. We're a hundred million light-years from home. We don't have time to waste on a tour!"

"That's where you're wrong, Matt," said Jess. "Our only chance of rescuing Snow and getting ourselves out of this game is to find out what makes

Granny Goose tick. Why not start with the tour? We'll walk around with the other visitors until we learn what we need to know. It'll be great cover. We can poke our noses anywhere. If someone asks questions, we're just a couple of dumb tourists who got lost."

"I don't know, Jess. Are you sure this can work?"

"Have I ever been wrong?"

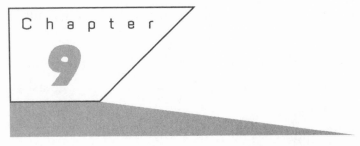

On the Air

Matt and Jess stepped out of the transporter into a large waiting area. "Is this where we start the tour?" Jess asked a receptionist sitting at a desk.

The young woman smiled. "It certainly is! Our last group left just a few minutes ago. If you hurry, you can catch up with them. Do you have studio tickets?"

"Uh, no!" said Matt.

"That's okay," she replied, sliding two tickets through the window. "There are two seats available in Studio Three-A. They're taping now. Would you like some chairs?"

"I didn't know you had to bring your own," Jess said.

"Oh, we have plenty of chairs for sitting. These are for something else."

"What?"

"You'll see. Enjoy the show."

Matt and Jess looked at each other and shrugged. They handed their tickets to the tour guide waiting at the door. "Three-A. Straight ahead on the right," he told them.

Lines were already forming in front of the studios. Jess and Matt saw people from all different parts of the world and others—if you could call them people—from different parts of the galaxy. Whether they were orange, purple, or green; whether they had one head or six; eight legs or two, they all carried folding chairs in their arms, grippers, claws, and tentacles.

"Isn't this exciting? I've never been on TV before," a kid thing with twelve eyes said to Jess.

"Really? I could have sworn I saw you on *Star Trek*," Jess answered. She wasn't able to say more than that because she felt Matt tugging at her sleeve.

"I don't think Snow is here," Matt whispered.

"Of course she's not here," Jess whispered back. "If we knew where she was, we'd be there. Chill, Matt! You can't lose your cool, or you'll blow the whole deal."

"I'm getting nervous."

"Just sit back and enjoy the show. Maybe they'll have prizes. We might win a refrigerator. Or a Hawaiian vacation. A real car! Then we could trade in the Tacomobile and—"

The studio doors opened. Matt and Jess picked up their chairs and followed the rest of the tour group inside. Studio assistants guided them to their seats. Matt and Jess had never been in a television studio before. They watched the cameras moving into position while the production assistants made last-minute adjustments to the set. It looked like an ordinary living room, except there seemed to be a lot of folding chairs.

Matt and Jess found themselves sitting between Xlaks, a lemrek from Pluto, and Hal, a retired fireman from Florida.

"Ain't this exciting!" said Hal. "I always wanted to be on the *Larry Zinger Show*."

"Me, too!" Xlaks buzzed. "I'm glad I have extra arms. I get to have extra chairs."

"Is this the *Larry Zinger Show*?" Jess and Matt both asked at once.

"It sure is! Why are you so surprised?"

"We're not allowed to watch it!"

"Too late for that now," said the fireman.

"We won't tell your parents," the lemrek promised.

Bright lights suddenly came on, lighting the set. The electronic sign overhead flashed APPLAUSE. Everybody in the audience began to clap and cheer.

"What are we clapping for?" Matt asked. He soon found out as a smiling man in a dark tie and blue blazer came on the set. He waved to the audience, and the crowd went wild. Everyone jumped from their seats, pumping their fists in the air.

"LAR-REE! LAR-REE! LAR-REE! LAR-REE! LAR-REE! LAR-REE!"

Jess and Matt jumped up, too, though it seemed odd to cheer for someone whose show they had never watched, one that their parents said was responsible for the decline of civilization.

"My mom says this show is the sewer of entertainment," Jess said.

"She's right!" Hal agreed. "Ain't it great?"

The electronic sign flashed SEATS. Everyone sat down as Larry Zinger took a hand mike from one of his assistants.

"Wow! What a terrific audience! And what a great show we have for you today. Any wrestling fans out there?"

The audience started yelling again, even before the electronic sign flashed.

"Then you're gonna love what we've got in store for you. Our guests today are three of the roughest, toughest, most beautiful ladies ever to wear spandex and leather. I'm talking about Miss Amazon, Miss Raven, and Miss Electra. They're gonna tell us all about THE SECRET LIVES OF WOMEN WRESTLERS!"

The electronic sign flashed APPLAUSE. The audience yelled, cheered, and whistled as Larry's three guests came onstage. Jessica gasped. Matt stared. He had never imagined that spandex could be stretched so tight, that hair could be piled so high, or that any human being could walk in thigh-high patent-leather boots with eight-inch stiletto heels. But these were no Buff Bikini Babes. They were more like Hard Bodies with Attitude. Their muscles rippled with the slightest movement, and the look on their perfectly made-up faces said, Get smart with me, Bozo, and I'll put you through the wall!

Miss Amazon wore a green costume and green hair, as if she were a spokesperson for the rain forest. Miss Raven preferred black, like a Halloween witch; and Miss Electra, the blonde, looked like Pamela Anderson on steroids. It was clear they weren't best friends. As they took their seats, they glared at one another like three cats gathered around an open can of Fiesta Feast.

"Welcome, ladies! It's a pleasure to have you on our show," Larry crowed as he exchanged kisses with each one. The audience hooted and hollered. "Here's a question I've been dying to ask. I'm sure the members of our audience have been wondering, too. How do athletes like yourselves, involved in the rough-and-tumble sport of Professional Women's Wrestling, retain your natural, unspoiled beauty?"

Miss Amazon spoke first. "Well, Larry, I think the answer to that question is the word *natural*. I drink only fruit juices, get plenty of sleep, eat lots of fruits and vegetables. I follow a natural diet and a natural lifestyle." Miss Raven began to giggle. "What are you laughing at, [bleep]!"

"I'm laughing at you, [bleep]! The only thing natural on you is your toenails. And I'm not sure about them."

"You're one to talk, Miss Frankenstein. Where did you find that Halloween outfit? At the kids' department at Kmart?"

Miss Electra jumped in, with a slow Southern drawl. "I hate to say this, sugar, but Amazon's right. The next time you want a makeover, Raven, honey, why don't you try visiting a beauty salon, not a funeral parlor."

Raven jumped out of her seat. She lunged at Miss Electra. "Don't talk to me about beauty salons, Miss Plastic Surgery! Everybody knows you don't dare stand near a radiator. You'd melt!"

"Why, you [bleep bleep bleep]!"

"Don't call me a [bleep], you [bleep]!"

The audience went berserk. "Fight! Fight!

Fight!" they screamed. The electronic sign flashed LOUDER!

"Now I know why Mom won't let me watch this show," Jess whispered to Matt.

"Why does anybody watch this show?" Matt whispered back.

By now Miss Raven and Miss Electra were locked in a screaming death match. Handfuls of black and blonde hair flew all over the set. Larry Zinger tried to break up the brawl. "Back off, Larry!" Amazon hollered. She backhanded him over the sofa, and when one of the security men tried to stop her, she whacked him with a chair. Electra and Raven stopped fighting and grabbed folding chairs, too. Soon it was the three women wrestlers, back to back like the Three Musketeers, taking on the whole production and security staff while the audience howled.

The electronic sign blinked CHAIRS! CHAIRS! CHAIRS! Everybody in the studio audience grabbed chairs and began whacking one another. They knocked over the cameras, demolished the set, tore down the curtains, smashed the lights in a riot of mass destruction.

"Let's get out of here before we're killed," Matt hollered to Jess.

Jess didn't want to leave. Matt had to drag her to the exit. "This is so cool!" she kept saying. A monitor beside the door recorded the brawl. A commercial break followed.

"This show is brought to you by Bilt-4-Komfort furniture—the chair that's made for more than sitting!"

"Where are you going? Don't you like the show?" a production assistant in the hallway asked. She carried a clipboard. "I'm Heather, by the way."

"Hi! I'm Jess. He's Matt. I love the show, but Matt thinks it's a little violent."

"Little!" Matt exclaimed.

"I suppose it might appear that way," Heather replied. "But no one ever really gets hurt. We're just giving the public what it wants."

"How do you know the public wants to see people whacking each other with chairs?" Matt asked.

"Granny Goose says so. And Granny knows. We all work for her. We do what she tells us."

"Or else?"

Heather didn't answer.

"Miss Heather, can I ask you a question?" Matt said. "If you could put together a TV show about anything at all, what would you choose?"

Heather paused to think. She smiled. "I'd do something about opera. I love opera."

"How about Mr. Zinger?"

"That's easy! The Civil War! He knows everything about it."

"And what about the three wrestlers: Miss Amazon, Miss Raven, and Miss Electra?" Jess asked.

Heather laughed. "Music! They're really great singers. They have this routine where they pretend to be the Supremes. Raven is Diana Ross. Amazon and Electra back her up as Flo and Mary. It's so tight! They know all the words and all the movements. You should see them do 'Stop in the Name of Love.' "

"Then they don't really hate each other?" asked Matt.

"Oh, no! It's just an act. They're completely different people when they're not on camera. So is Mr. Zinger. So am I. So is everyone else at Universe Studios. I guess we're all pretending to be something we're not."

"That's too bad," said Matt.

"We try not to think about it," Heather replied. "There's nothing we can do. Granny holds all the cards. Or should I say . . . cookies?" A wistful look crossed Heather's face, but only for a moment. She smiled. "Perhaps you'd like to visit our recording studios. Several new groups are recording today." She checked the clipboard. "Let's see . . . Los Kangaroos . . . Possum Death . . . No Fairy Tales! Oh, no!"

Jess looked at Matt. Matt looked back. Neither said anything.

"No Fairy Tales. They sound cool," said Matt.

"Don't you like them?" Jess asked Heather.

"I love them!" Heather replied. "They're my favorite underground group. I have all their CDs. Did you ever hear 'Road Kill Wolf'?"

"Uh . . . that rings a bell," said Jess.

"Yeah," Matt added. "We might have heard it when we were driving here."

"If you heard it, you'd remember it—big time!" said Heather. "But I guess No Fairy Tales won't be recording anything like that anymore. I imagine they won't even be No Fairy Tales after today."

"Why not?"

"Granny always makes the groups change their names. Our groups record what Granny tells them. Granny selects their songs. Granny chooses their costumes. She creates their whole image. Granny writes the script, and our job is to follow it. If we do what Granny tells us, we live happily ever after."

"What's wrong with that?" Matt asked.

"It's not real," said Heather. "If you're not real, you can't really be happy. And no one is ever going to be happy again if Granny Goose controls everything in the universe."

"That's right, Miss Heather. Granny does control everything in the universe. And don't you forget it!" Granny Goose's sour face filled the overhead monitor. "Now get back to work! As for you two little creeps, didn't I say I wanted you in my office? Where have you been? I'm getting tired of waiting."

"Hi, Granny!" Jess said. "We got off at the wrong floor."

"We figured we'd take in the studio tour as long as we were here," Matt added.

"Well, you figured wrong! Tour's over. I want you upstairs, pronto! And just to make sure you don't get lost again. . . ." Jess and Matt felt immensely strong cyber-fingers clamp onto their shoulders. They looked up into the video screen faces of two yo'bots. Gangsta One and 6-Pak glared down at them.

Jess and Matt sighed. "Busted again!"

"Move it, homes," the yo'bots growled. "You don't wanna keep Granny waiting."

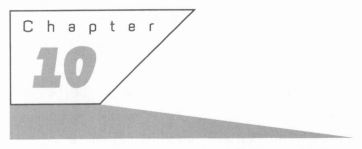

Chapter

10

Central Processing

The yo'bots marched Jess and Matt to the transporters. Gangsta One pressed the button. The doors
opened, but the yo'bots didn't move. Jess glanced
up at the video screen. 6-Pak had vanished. In his
place stood a beautiful blonde model demonstrating
an exercise machine.

"Come on, Matt!" Jess yelled. She grabbed
Matt's wrist and pulled him into the transporter.
The yo'bots stood motionless as the transporter
doors closed. Jess frantically hit all the buttons
on the screen. The transporter zoomed through

the conveyer tube, leaving the yo'bots far behind.

"What was that all about?" Matt gasped. "Why didn't the yo'bots stop us?"

"Remember what Snow told us in the Tacomobile? Yo'bots break for commercials. When commercials come on, they go into Sleep mode."

"Where are we going now?"

"You'll see," Jess answered. "Heather helped us a lot. I definitely have a better picture of what we're up against. Granny is forcing Snow and her band to record her kind of music. Snow knew that Granny was trying to track her down. That's why the band split up after the concert—they figured they'd be harder to catch if they separated. Snow must have been the last one to fall into Granny's hands. Once Granny had the whole band in her clutches, she could go ahead and schedule a recording session. The question now is, what do we do about it?"

"Any ideas?"

"A couple," said Jess. She laid out her plan to Matt as the transporter stopped at several floors in succession. "Here's where we get off. Let's go!"

———

The sign on the wall read CENTRAL PROCESSING. Matt looked around at the pipes and wiring that snaked along the corridor ceiling.

"This doesn't look like Central Processing. It's more like our basement at home."

"Listen to that humming. I can feel the vibrations through the floor. There's some kind of machinery down here. Let's check it out." Jess led Matt along the corridor. They passed a sign that said GRANNY'S COOKIE JAR. An arrow pointed ahead, in the direction they were going.

"What do you suppose that means?" Matt asked.

"It means we're on the right track. Let me know when you start smelling chocolate chips," said Jess. They followed the signs around a corner. The corridor ended before a massive double door as solid as the entrance to a bank vault. Two muscular SWAT'bots in camouflage uniforms manned the security booth. They turned to Matt and Jess. Terminator CXXVIII flickered across their face screens.

"Clearance?" #1 asked in Arnold's thick German accent.

"Granny sent us," said Matt.

"We need to check the cookies," Jess added.

"Proceed," said #2 in Arnold's voice. The SWAT'-bot pushed a button. The doors silently opened.

"Granny needs to beef up her security. These guys are brain dead," Jess whispered to Matt. "We may rescue Snow and win this game yet."

They found themselves in a giant hall filled with computers. Tapes whirred, disks clicked, hard drives hummed, lasers flashed on and off.

"I get it!" said Matt. "Granny's Cookie Jar is one huge server. This is where she stores and tabulates the data she gathers from her cookies."

Jess gasped in awe. "Hundreds of millions of cookies, feeding her information about every individual in the universe who's ever gone online. Wow! You could rule the cosmos with ten percent of that."

"One percent," Matt agreed.

Jessica walked around, trying to take it all in. "How does she catalog all that information? How does she access it?"

"The same way we find information on the Web. She must use some kind of search engine."

"How? I don't see any monitors," Jess said. "There's only that phone on the wall."

"There's probably a network that lets her access what she needs from anywhere on the planet," Matt said.

"But someone must come down here for maintenance. People have to get into the computers to service them," Jess insisted. "The SWAT'bots didn't think there was anything unusual about our coming down here to 'check the cookies.' There has to be a way."

"Maybe they bring their own laptops and plug them into the system," Matt suggested.

Jess shrieked. "That's it! The missing piece! The last clue!" She threw her arms around Matt and gave him a big kiss. "You're a genius! I'm going to write Britney myself to tell her what a cool guy you are!"

Matt blushed bright red. "Huh? What did I say?"

"Laptops!" said Jess. "The cookies are the key to the game, and laptops are the key to the cookies. It's all falling into place. We have everything we need now. Leave the rest to me." She picked up the phone. "Hello? Excuse me. I hate to bother you guys, but we came in here a few minutes ago to check the cookies. The service department told us there was a laptop down here. We can't find it." Jess listened. "Okay. Aisle five. Go down past the rest rooms and the pop machine. On the right. Got it. Thanks, Arnold!" Jess hung up the phone. "You were right, Matt. On the button! Aisle five. Follow me!"

All the aisles were clearly marked, so Jess and Matt had no trouble finding Aisle five. They hurried along past banks of blinking, whirring computers.

"All systems go?" Matt asked.

"You bet! Granny's goose is cooked. She doesn't know it yet, but her little red plastic button is about to pop. We're in the final stretch, Matt. Ready, set, here we go!"

They found the laptop exactly where the SWAT'bot said it would be. They didn't even have to turn it on. Jessica touched a key. The screen came to life, displaying the menu.

"Here's **<Search>**," said Matt. Jess clicked on the button. When **<Find>** appeared, Jessica typed in

<Granny Goose/Personal File> and hit **<Enter>**. The monitor darkened. The planetary image of Universe Studios filled the screen, with the words *Searching . . . Searching . . .* revolving around the rings.

"It's taking a long time," said Matt. "What do you suppose we'll find?"

"Plenty!" said Jess.

The screen came back to life. Beneath the words **<Search Results>** were page after page of information. As Jess and Matt scrolled through, their eyes grew wider and wider.

"Granny's toast!" said Matt.

"Burnt toast!" Jess agreed. "I just have a few little details to finish up." Her fingers danced across the keyboard. "Okay, we're done here. Now let's find Snow."

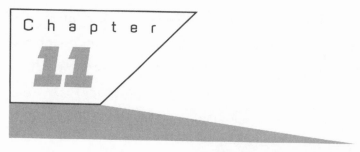

C h a p t e r

11

All the Cookies

"I'm sorry, guys. I just can't do it." Snow paced back and forth across the recording studio. "These costumes! This music! I can't go through with it."

Cindi picked an encouraging riff on her Stratocaster. "C'mon, Snow! You gotta try. You heard what Granny told us. You know what's at stake. If we don't agree to perform the music she wants, we all go back to the Land of Fairy Tales. Without the happy ending."

Red filled in with a drumroll. "Okay, the costumes are dorky. I'd still rather wear a ridiculous costume than be locked up in the tower with that paranoid old witch. She wouldn't even let me use the phone!"

"It's better than being pushed around by fat, stupid stepsisters," Cindi agreed.

"Or having to kiss a guy with more hair on his face than I have on my head," said Beauty.

"Or being mauled by a wolf," Red added. "I don't believe that creep! He kept trying to get into bed with my grandma!"

"Sure!" sniffed Snow, looking at her image in the mirror with deep disgust. The blue jumpsuit, white platform shoes, flowered headband, and frilly lace blouse definitely recalled an earlier era in the history of rock music. Unfortunately, it was an era that no one was dying to bring back. "Can't you see it? We'll travel to gigs in a cute little bus like the Partridge Family. We'll have our own little Fairy-Tale Band cartoon show on Saturday morning. We'll be on the cover of *Teen Scene*. We'll perform duets with Barney. We'll make—"

Beauty interrupted Snow's tirade with a familiar

run on the bass. "I can't get no . . . satisfaction!"

"Okay, what are you saying?" said Snow.

"What I'm saying," Beauty began, "is that we don't have a choice. I'd rather be in a bubble-gum band than no band at all. If we don't go through with it, Granny calls the reporters and spreads our cookies all over the media. We'll be the laughing-stock of the universe. I, for one, don't want it known that my former brother-in-law is a lion in the San Diego Zoo."

"Or that my fairy godmother is a cross-dresser," Cindi chimed in.

"Or that the prince gave me head lice," said Punzi.

"Or that the basket of goodies I was bringing to Grandma's house was full of cigars and whiskey." Red twirled a drumstick, flipped it in the air, and caught it behind her back. "We all have secrets, Snow. Let's make sure they stay secrets. Unless you don't mind going back to the dwarfs?"

Snow shuddered. "Okay, Granny wins. From the top . . ." She took the lyric sheets from the music stand, clamped the headphones over her ears, and began singing:

"If you want to be with me,

Honey, there's a price to pay.

You have to get a job.

It is the only way.

I am not supporting you

(Though you may not think that's fair)

Just so you can hang around

In your underwear . . ."

Snow threw off the headphones. "Sorry. I can't sing this. It's mega-crudito!"

"It has a good message. Chicks shouldn't let dudes sponge off them," Red interrupted.

"I don't care. You can spray kitty litter with perfume and gift wrap it. It's still—"

The recording studio door flew open. Two kids tumbled in, followed by three large women with bulging biceps who looked like cartoon superheroes come to life.

"Matt! Jess! What are you doing here?" Snow exclaimed.

"We just came from the TV studio. We brought some singers for your session," said Jess. "We thought you might need some backup."

Amazon, Raven, and Electra began squealing. "Ooooooo! It's Snow White and her band! Can we be in your group? No Fairy Tales! Eeeeeeeeee!"

"They're really good," said Matt. "You should hear them do 'Love Child.' "

"Weren't you just on the *Larry Zinger Show*?" Punzi asked.

"Yeah," Amazon replied. "The show ended early."

"We ended it." Raven and Electra winked at each other.

"Thanks, sisters. I'm sure you're terrific. But the band and I need more than backup singers to get us out of this mess," said Snow. "We need—"

"You need to get back to work and finish the record so we can start filming the video." An all-too-familiar face filled the overhead monitor screen.

"Hi, Granny!" said Jess. "Bake any COOKIES lately?"

"What are you doing here? I want you and Matt in my office now! Or do I have to send some more 'bots to show you the way?"

Matt giggled. "Don't bother. You won't find any. They're on vacation." Matt picked up the channel selector and pressed a button that split the monitor screen in two. MTV's *Spring Break in Puerta Vallarta* came on to fill the second portion. Yo'bots and SWAT'bots in bathing suits and sunglasses filled the beach, surrounded by several hundred Buff Bikini Babes. Two of the 'bots grinned into the camera.

"Yo! This is Love Machine, and I'm here with my home'bot, Arnold. We're sending love and peace to everybody at Universe Studios. Except that [bleep!] Granny Goose, who paid us nothing and worked us like robots! Drop dead, Granny!"

"Ja! You vouldn't giff us a vacation. So ve took one. Ve got in der pods and left!"

"We're having a blast down here! Our *fun* in the *sun* has just be*gun*!"

"Right on, bro! *Hasta la vista*, Granny. Ve von't be back!"

Jess clicked back to the full screen. "I thought the 'bots might like a holiday, so I reprogrammed them while Matt and I were down in Central Processing."

"Why, you little twerps! How dare you hack into my files!"

"We didn't hack, Granny," said Matt. "Your security is a joke. We entered your name, and the search engine gave us everything we wanted. You should look into getting a fire wall. Or at least a password."

"As long as we're talking computers, Granny," said Jess, "there's something else I want to ask. How come you know so much about everybody in the universe, but nobody knows anything about you?"

"Because I'm the Cookie Master. I control all the secrets."

"Did you say Master, or Monster? Why don't you come out of the closet? Maybe I'll be able to hear you better."

"What are you talking about?"

"That closet. Over there." Jess pointed to a door marked CLEANING SUPPLIES—KEEP OUT! "It's like the Wizard of Oz," she continued. "The real wizard was hiding behind the curtain. And the real Granny Goose is hiding in that closet."

"You're wrong! It's all lies! Don't believe her!" Granny began yelling.

"I know one way to find out," said Amazon, turning the doorknob. "Aw, it's locked!"

"Too bad," said Electra as she ripped the door off its hinges. The three women wrestlers charged into the closet. Terrible sounds of equipment overturning, wires sparking, and monitors exploding came through the door. Raven, Electra, and Amazon emerged moments later, dragging out a tiny old lady in a calico dress.

"Granny Goose, I presume," said Matt.

Granny looked from Matt to Jess to Snow. "Tell them not to hurt me! You better let me go. I may not have any 'bots, but I still have plenty on all of you. I'll spill the whole cookie jar. I will!"

"Really?" said Jess. "Like you told *ET* that Raven's engagement to The Stone was off?"

"What!" sobbed Raven. "You leaked the story before I had a chance to tell him. I ought to smash you!"

Jess went on. "Or tipping off CNN that Amazon was secretly dating Smashin' Sam Dallas?"

Amazon shrieked. "So you're the one! I could squash you for that!"

"How about letting *People* magazine know that Electra gained a few pounds over Christmas and was having trouble fitting into her costume?"

Electra fixed Granny Goose with a look of cold fury. "Stand back, girls! She's mine. I'm gonna kill her."

"Yeah! It's time for . . . Slapdown!"

"Do something, Jess. They really will kill her," Matt whispered.

"Hold on, everybody!" Jess said. Red backed her up with a drumroll and a clash of cymbals. "Granny Goose knows plenty of secrets about us. I think it's time we opened the jar and doled out some of her cookies. How would you all like to learn something about our dear old Granny?"

"Yeah!" everyone in the studio cried.

"Well, here it is. Granny Goose is a fake. She doesn't exist. She isn't old, and she isn't a granny. Granny Goose is a guy! Or should I say . . . dwarf!"

"What!" Raven grabbed Granny in a hammerlock. Amazon pulled off her wig and mask. Electra ripped off her dress. Underneath was indeed a dwarf! And not just any dwarf. Matt instantly recognized the crumpled suit and stained tie.

"Sleazy!"

"Give it up," said Jess. "We've got you cold!"

"Okay, you win," Sleazy confessed. "I'm Granny

Goose. I flooded the Web with ultraviolent games to get parents worried. Then I started pushing the Fun Farm. Either way, I ended up with cookies from all the gamers in the universe. Same with TV. I flooded the market with junk to drive out the good shows, then I brought them back, but under my terms. I was gonna do the same with music, except I needed a hit group. That's where Snow White and her band came in. Too bad you spoiled my plan. They could have been bigger than the Jacksons!"

"Yuck!" said Snow and all her friends. "Where'd you get the money for all this?" Snow demanded.

"Diamonds," Sleazy told her. "I was working a crooked dice game in Narnia when I learned that my seven brothers were squashed in a cave-in. I inherited the family diamond mine. I sold it to your stepmother for a bundle and invested the profits in shady dot-coms. The magic mirror warned me to get out before the market collapsed. I made a killing. I invested the profits in media and telecommunication companies, which were at rock bottom. Soon I controlled studios, broadcasting stations, research labs all over the universe. Yo'bots and SWAT'bots gave me muscle when I needed it. Most of the time I got what I wanted with plain cold cash."

"So where did Matt and I fit in?" Jess asked.

"Nowhere. I was sitting around with nothing to do the day you and your buddy walked into the Fun Farm. I should have left you alone. You would have found your way out sooner or later. That was my downfall. I love messing with people's heads."

"Well, your messing days are over," Matt said. "You're in big trouble with the FCC, the ICC, the FBI, the CIA, and the UN, and a couple of dozen intergalactic and interplanetary agencies. Even if you don't go to jail, by the time you get done paying your lawyers, you're going to be back rolling those loaded dice."

"Or panhandling in the park," said Jess.

"Or working in my stepmom's diamond mine, digging for zircons," said Snow.

"In your dreams, baby! Hate to disappoint you all, but I have other plans." Sleazy wiggled out of his sport jacket and raced for the door. He ran surprisingly fast for such a little person. But he didn't get far. Years of late-night poker games, fatty fried foods, and cheap cigars quickly began to tell.

Panting and wheezing, Sleazy threw himself up against a door marked STUDIO X.

"You're finished, Sleazy!" Amazon shouted. "Give it up while you still have a chance."

"I know what you're thinking!" Heather cried. "Don't go in there, Sleazy! Please! There must be another way!"

"You'll never take me alive!" Sleazy yanked open the door and dashed inside. An unearthly scream echoed down the corridor.

"Oh no! Sleazy ran into Studio X!" Heather sobbed.

"What's Studio X?" Jess and Matt asked.

"That's where we process . . . THE RERUNS!"

Chapter

12

Happily Ever After

"Home at last!" Jess exclaimed. She looked around at the posters on the walls of her room. Never had she seen a more welcome sight.

"Yeah," Matt agreed. "That was a great idea Heather had, sending us back as e-mail attachments."

"I'm going downstairs to tell Mom we finished the game. For good!" As Jess ran down the stairs, she met her mother coming up.

"Hi, hon! I hope you're not still playing that game. If you are, I want you to stop. Immediately!"

"Why?"

"Because **www.grannysworld.com** isn't as innocent as it looks. I don't ever want you to visit that website again. It has links to weird cults and Neo-Nazi hate sites. Click on Harvey Hamster, and he starts giving one of Adolf Hitler's speeches. In German!"

"Whoa!" said Jess. "Where did you find that out?"

"On a fascinating new talk show called *Heather's World*. I know, you're going to ask why I'm watching TV when I told you to turn it off. It's been a tough day at the hospital. I needed to veg out before I started dinner. I'm glad I did, because otherwise I never would have discovered that wonderful show. You'll be glad, too. Because Heather taught me that I was completely wrong about computer games. Children who play violent computer games are *less* likely to engage in actual violence themselves. They also get better grades, have better social relationships, and are friendlier and more cooperative at home and in school than their peers. I guess you were right, Jess. Computer games *are* good for you. So I'm returning your games, and I also want to ask a favor. I'd like you to play them at least one hour a day."

"Sure, Mom! I can handle that," said Jess. She winked up at Matt. *Thanks, Heather,* she thought.

"That sounds like a good show. Who else was on?" Matt asked.

"The Three Tenors. They sang arias from famous operas, then shared their favorite recipes. They made enough tomato sauce to float a battleship. Larry Zinger was next. He knew all about the Civil War. It was nice to see him have a discussion without throwing chairs. Then three women wrestlers came on, singing songs of the sixties. They were very good. I didn't like the last guests, though. Five young women from some retro–New Wave band. They didn't sing; they just screamed! Why can't they sing wholesome, positive songs?"

"Like the Partridge Family?" Matt suggested.

"Yes, like the Partridges. That was such a good show. Speaking of TV, have either of you watched *The Grady Bunch* lately?"

"No," said Jess. "Why?"

"It's very strange. This horrible little man seems

to have moved into the Grady House. At first I thought he was one of Alice's boyfriends, but Alice can't stand him. He keeps trying to put the moves on Marcia. Greg dumped him in the garbage can and left him on the curb with the trash, but he was back for the next episode. Do you know anything about him?"

"Not a thing!" Matt and Jess said.

"See if there's something on the Web. Let me know what you find out." Jess's mom went back downstairs to prepare dinner.

Matt looked at Jess. Jess looked at Matt. They heard a familiar theme song playing on the TV in the family room. Except the words were different.

"Here's the story . . . of a dwarf named Sleazy . . ."

"Poor Sleazy!" said Matt.

"Poor Gradys!" Jess sighed. "They'll never get rid of him now."

Because as every TV watcher knows . . .

Reruns are forever!